W9-BJT-373

DISCARDED
From Nashville Public Library

LEGO CITY

LOOK OUT BELOW!

By Michael Anthony Steele
Illustrated by Kenny Kiernan

SCHOLASTIC INC.

Nashville Public Library
Nashville Public Library

No part of this publication may be reproduced in whole or in part, stored in a retrieval system, or transmitted in any form or by any means, electronic, mechanical, photocopying, recording, or otherwise, without written permission of the publisher. For information regarding permission, write to Scholastic Inc., Attention: Permissions Department, 557 Broadway, New York, NY 10012.

ISBN 978-0-545-41555-2

LEGO, the LEGO logo, the Brick and Knob configurations and the Minifigure are trademarks of the LEGO Group. © 2012 The LEGO Group. Produced by Scholastic Inc. under license from the LEGO Group.

All rights reserved. Published by Scholastic Inc. SCHOLASTIC and associated logos are trademarks and/or registered trademarks of Scholastic Inc.
Lexile is a registered trademark of MetaMetrics.

12 11 10 9 8 7 6 5 4 40
Designed by Angela Jun
Printed in the U.S.A.
First printing, July 2012

13 14 15 16 17/0

Hoot!
The work whistle blows.
George and Johnny arrive at the gold mine.

The trucks are filled with rocks.
The rocks have gold inside.

"Gold mining really rocks!" Johnny cheers.

George and Johnny ride in a cart.
Everyone wears safety gear.

"We better rush to get that gold," Johnny says.
HB 2846

Rummmmble!
A drill digs the large tunnels.

"I really dig that drill," says Johnny.

George uses a jackhammer.
It breaks apart the large rocks.

The boulders are loaded onto a trailer.

"Let's rock and roll," says Johnny.

The trailer goes out of the tunnel.

The miners take a break.
They eat sandwiches.

"My bread is as hard as a rock," says George.

One miner reaches for a drink. He bumps into a lantern.

"Be careful!" George shouts.

"Good thing we have our head lamps," says George.

"Let's head out of here," says Johnny.

Johnny fixes the lamp.

He looks at the wall where the lamp fell.

There is gold in the rock.

"Let's blast a new tunnel over here," says Johnny.

George sets the timer.

Then everyone leaves the mine.

Boom!
The ground shakes.
SECURITY

"This job is a blast!" Johnny says.
GOLD MINE
STOP

The dust settles.
Everyone returns to the mine.

"Look at all that gold," says George.

"We rock!" says Johnny.

BUILD YOUR LEGO® LIBRARY!

SCHOLASTIC and associated logos are trademarks and/or registered trademarks of Scholastic Inc. LEGO, the LEGO logo, the Brick and Knob configurations and the Minifigure are trademarks of the LEGO Group. © 2012 The LEGO Group. Produced by Scholastic Inc. under license from the LEGO Group.

SCHOLASTIC

scholastic.com
LEGO.com

LEGOCT